Michael Grejniec

Good Morning,

Good Night

North-South Books   New York

It is dark.

It is light.

Good morning.

I am inside.

I am outside.

I am hiding.

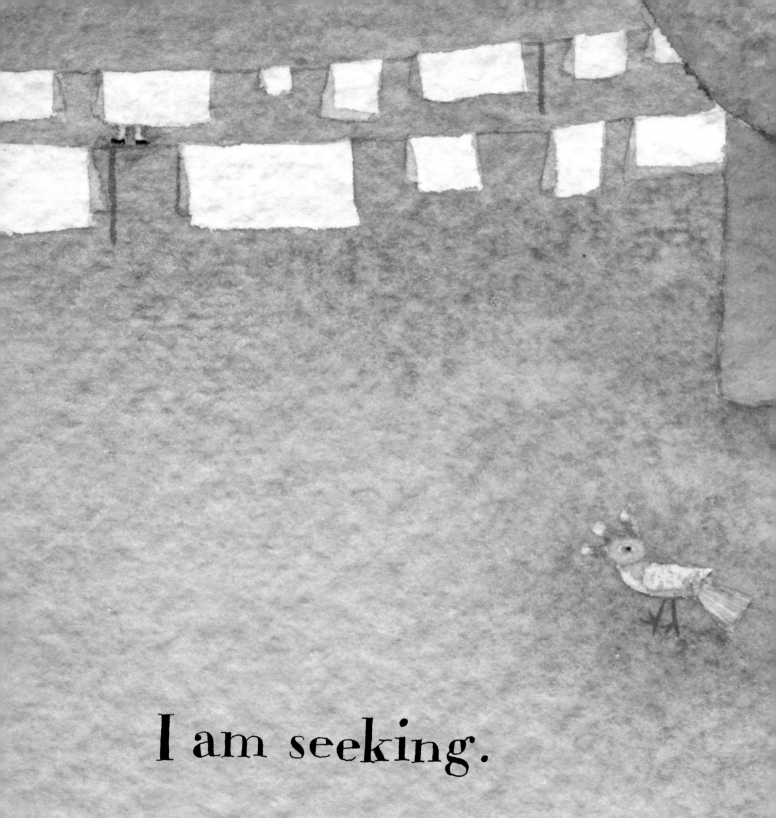

I am seeking.

I have one.

I have many.

I am low.

I am high.

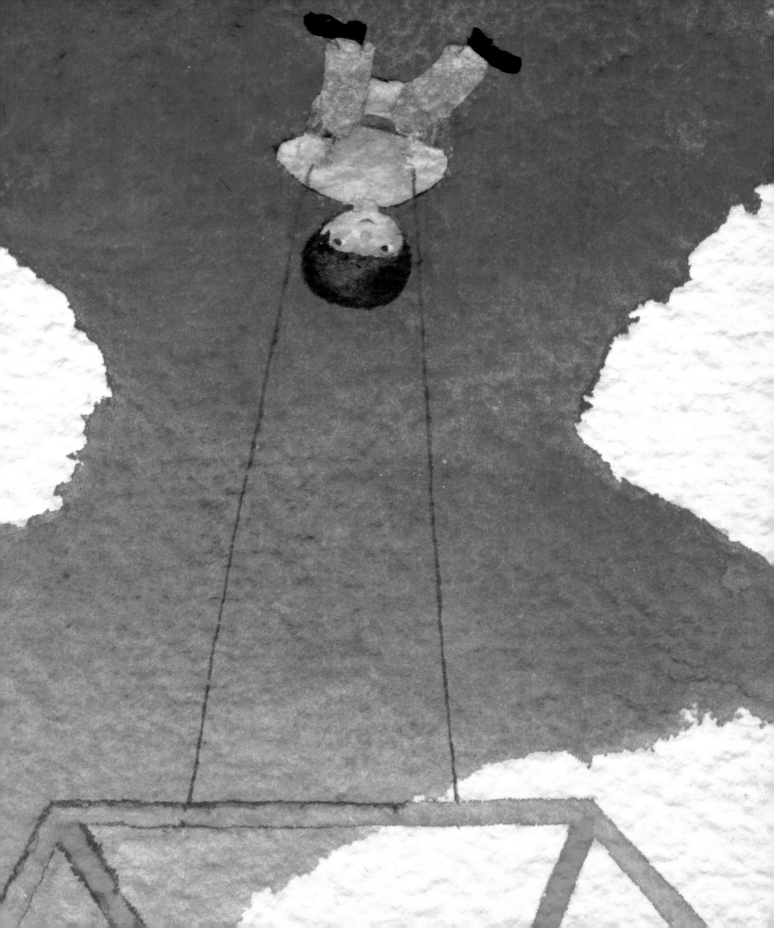

It is quiet.

It is noisy.

We are far.

We are close.

Good night.

Copyright © 1993 by Michael Grejniec

All rights reserved.
No part of this book may be reproduced or utilized in any form
or by any means, electronic or mechanical, including photocopying,
recording, or any information storage and retrieval system,
without permission in writing from the publisher.

Published in the United States by North-South Books Inc., New York.

Published simultaneously in Great Britain, Canada,
Australia, and New Zealand in 1993 by North-South Books,
an imprint of Nord-Süd Verlag AG, Gossau Zürich, Switzerland.

Library of Congress Cataloging-in-Publication Data
Grejniec, Michael.
Good morning, good night / Michael Grejniec.
Summary: Two children in a day of play experience such opposites as
inside and outside, hiding and seeking, and low and high.
ISBN 1-55858-173-1 (trade binding)
ISBN 1-55858-174-X (library binding)
[1. English language—Synonyms and antonyms—Fiction.] I. Title.
PZ7.G8625Go   1993
[E]—dc20   92-23530

A CIP catalogue record for this book
is available from The British Library

1 3 5 7 9 10 8 6 4 2
Printed in Belgium

The art was painted with Pelican and Windsor Newton
watercolors on Colombe paper. The color separations were made
from transparencies, rather than the original art, so that the texture
of the watercolor paper would appear in the printed book. All
the images were enlarged 250%, to accentuate the details
and the rough edges of the painting.

Book design and hand lettering
by Michael Grejniec